Mia and the Lost Voice

©© 2021 Anthony Baptiste
Published by scribsalots

All Rights reserved

No part of this book may be reproduced in any form or by any electronic or mechanical means, including information storage and retrieval systems, without permission in writing from the author or publisher, except by reviewers, who may quote brief passages in a review

ISBN 9781838370381

Contact me: Anthony
twitter: @scribsalots
email: scribsalots@gmail.com

Dedicated to my rock, my base, my family and friend's network.

Special mention to the staff and pupils of The Rissington School

The pitter-patter of tiny footsteps crossing the floor caught mum's attention. They were slow and not hurried at all, letting mum know that something wasn't right.

Mia had a look of discomfort on her dark honey-coloured face, and her mother knew right away that something was not right.

"Are you ok, darling?" said mum, worry creeping into her voice. Mia tried to reply, but no words came out.

"Oh no, Mia, you have lost it, again?" said mum, her voice wavering just a little bit.

Holding her neck, Mia cocked her head to one side of her lanky body and nodded. Mia tried again to speak with no luck. A large tear rolled down her cheek. Quickly her sadness turned to frustration as she started to realize that losing her voice was happening often. This made her anxious it was going away for good. She shook her head and stamped her foot. Her thick black hair waved from side to side. That one tear had grown into a solid stream before she finally placed her head on mummy's shoulder.

"I was hoping we didn't have to go back so soon," Mia heard mum say almost to herself. "Come on, let's go see Doctor Rose and see if she can help us find your voice again."

Mia was determined to get her voice back as they jumped in the car. She focused her brown eyes on the road ahead. Nothing was going to distract her today. Not the playful puppy in the neighbour's garden. Nor the moody cows grazing in the field.

The doctor looked for Mia's voice everywhere. She looked deep inside her ear with a cold shinny thing. She looked down her throat with a bright light. There was even a quick peek up her nose. She even checked her chest and back. Doctor Rose look and she looked but Mia's voice was nowhere to be found.

"Hmmm," she said, tapping her doctorly finger on her left cheek, "Yes, it may take a little while, but her voice will come back," she said.

This was not comforting news to Mia or her mother. They left Doctor Rose's office disappointed and wondering how long it might take to get her voice back this time.

The next day Mia heard mum talking on the phone. She wondered who mummy was talking to. She would usually ask but this time she had no voice at all.

"Yes, it's happened again, we'll see you on Sunday" she heard mummy say.

Mia knew it was granny and that she was going to visit this Sunday. She grew excited. Over the next few days, she thought of how she could get her voice back. On Wednesday when her mother was finished reading her big red medicine book Mia hid under the blanket and looked at the pictures. No voice was hiding in there but there were lots of strange pictures. Mia spent most of the time wishing her voice would return as she sat quietly drawing or building castles with brightly coloured bricks.

It had been a few days since Mia saw Dr. Rose, and she still didn't have her voice back. Tomorrow her grandmother would be visiting. Most Sundays Mia and Grandma watched cartoons together. They joked and laughed while they watched their favourite characters get into all sorts of funny situations.

"Oh no," thought Mia. "Grandma is coming over tomorrow, and I won't be able to talk to her."

She really loved talking to grandma. She had to do something. "I'll find my voice all by myself and right away," she thought.

She started in the living room. Maybe her voice was hiding there. She looked behind the sofa. It was dark, and her eyes strained to see, but all she found were crumbs and a few coins that had fallen out of someone's pocket. No voice, at least not yet.

She next looked under her bed. She found her lost toy duck and her red comb, but no voice anywhere to be seen.

She climbed onto the bed and pulled back the sheets. Maybe it had fallen out of her while she was sleeping, but again no voice was there.

Disappointed and out of places to look, Mia buried herself in her favourite green blanket and tried to think hard about where she might look for her missing voice. All that thinking was making her tired, and before she knew it, she had fallen fast asleep.

She dreamed that she was riding her bike in the park when suddenly she heard something familiar. The sound of her voice was coming from the top of a giant tree in the park. Her eyebrows shot up! Why was her voice inside that tree? There were many other strange sounds in the tree. Noisy squawking, soothing cooing, strange groaning and creaking all came from this green giant with branches swaying in the wind as clouds raced by in the blue sky. It seemed this tree had enough of its own voices. It certainly didn't need hers too!

In her dream, she rode her bike straight up the tree trunk. She peddled past colourful birds and swaying branches, past the squawking and the cooing, getting closer and closer to the sound of her own voice.

In the middle of the tree, she could hear her voice coming from a large dark hole in the tree trunk. It was dark and reminded her of the space behind the sofa. The hole in the tree was a little darker and a whole lot scarier.

She put one hand into the hole and pulled it out quickly. Her hand was shaking. She tried again, this time ignoring her racing heart, and she put her entire shaking arm into the hole. It seemed to grow larger the further her arm went in. It was so dark and big she almost fell inside! She could feel there was something there, but she just did not know what it was. Moving her arm about she grabbed a small, warm, fluffy ball and held it up to see.

It bounced in her hand and said, "Mia! You found me Mia! I am your voice! I got lost in this tree, and I have been so scared without you!" Mia smiled triumphantly.

"Mia... Mia," she heard in the distance.

Opening her sleepy eyes slowly, she found that she was no longer in the park. It must have been a dream. She was in bed, where she had curled up with her blanket, but she was laying crookedly in her bed, and her covers were all twisted. As she started to realize she had been dreaming, the excitement of finding her voice was fading.

"Whatever were you dreaming about, darling? You were kicking like crazy in your sleep! Look, your blanket is half on the floor," mum said, laughing.

"So, Little Miss Mia, are you hungry?"

"Yes. Very hungry mummy," said Mia.

"Oh, oh, oh!" mum said. "Your voice is... is back!" mum hugged Mia tightly.

"Mummy, I found my voice," said Mia. "I rode my bike up the tree and found my voice hiding in a big hole."

"Ok, darling," mum said in amusement.

Little Mia was very proud of herself. Her belly had a voice of its own as it rumbled. Mum had made Mia's favourite green vegetable soup, which had a loud voice of its very own. Ding Dong! The doorbell rang, and grandma stood at the front door. Mia could not wait to tell her about how she found her voice in the tree.

The End.

COLOUR ME

DRAW ME

Read the next two in this exciting series

Mia and the Amazing Spots

And

Mia's New Best Friend

Printed in Great Britain
by Amazon